SHORT TALES
Furlock & Muttson Mysteries

The Case of
THE MYSTERY MUSEUM

by Robin Koontz

visit us at www.abdopublishing.com

Published by Magic Wagon, a division of the ABDO Group, 8000 West 78th Street, Edina, Minnesota, 55439. Copyright © 2010 by Abdo Consulting Group, Inc. International copyrights reserved in all countries. All rights reserved. No part of this book may be reproduced in any form without written permission from the publisher.

Short Tales ™ is a trademark and logo of Magic Wagon.

Printed in the United States of America, North Mankato, Minnesota.
092009
012010

 PRINTED ON RECYCLED PAPER

Written and illustrated by Robin Koontz
Edited by Stephanie Hedlund and Rochelle Baltzer
Interior Layout by Kristen Fitzner Denton
Book Design and Packaging by Shannon Eric Denton

Library of Congress Cataloging-in-Publication Data

Koontz, Robin Michal.
  The case of the mystery museum / written and illustrated by Robin Koontz.
    p. cm. -- (Short tales. Furlock & Muttson mysteries)
  ISBN 978-1-60270-562-3
  [1. Museums--Fiction. 2. Mystery and detective stories.] I. Title.
  PZ7.K83574Casn 2010
  [E]--dc22
                                    2008032497

"Muttson, look here!" Furlock said. "There is
a new show at the museum today!"
"What is the show?" Muttson asked.

"Ancient fish fossils!" said Furlock.
"Old fish bones," Muttson groaned.
"Very well, I will fire up the Furlock-
Mobile."

There was a long line at the museum.
"I am not the only one who likes old fish bones," Furlock said.
"So I see," said Muttson.

Just then, Mr. Leon appeared in the doorway.
"Everyone please go home," he said. "The new show
will not open today."
"Why not?" cried Furlock.

"Because we have a mystery," said Mr. Leon.
"Then we are here just in time!" Furlock said.
"Furlock and Muttson Detective Agency,
at your service."

"Please come in," said Mr. Leon. "I hope you can solve this mystery!"
Furlock and Muttson followed Mr. Leon to the gem and mineral room.

"This case was filled with gems," said Mr. Leon.
"Many of the gems are missing."
Muttson snapped a photo.

"Was the case locked?" asked Furlock.
"No," said Mr. Leon. "But we do lock the doors and windows."
"Is anything else missing?" asked Furlock.

"Follow me," said Mr. Leon.
Furlock and Muttson followed Mr. Leon to the
fossil room.
"The ancient fish fossils!" said Furlock.

"Yes," said Mr. Leon. "And the smallest one is missing."
He pointed to an empty stand.
"Oh dear!" cried Furlock.

"Is anything else missing?" Muttson asked.
"Follow me," said Mr. Leon.
Furlock and Muttson followed Mr. Leon to
the American history room.

"Look at our live river display," said
Mr. Leon. "The gold nuggets are missing."
Furlock pointed at a large mound.

"What is that?" she asked.
"That is a thousand-year-old midden," said
Mr. Leon. "The ancient home of a pack rat."

"Look at all the stuff in there," said Furlock.
"Pack rats like to collect bones, seeds,
and shiny things," said Mr. Leon.

"We learn about history from their middens," he said.
Muttson snapped photos of the midden and the river display.

"Where is the light coming from?" Furlock
asked.
"The skylight," said Mr. Leon.
"I need a stool, please!" said Furlock.

"You may use the midden," said Mr. Leon.
Furlock climbed on the midden.
"Aha!" she said. "This is how the thief got
inside."

"Oh dear!" said Mr. Leon. "We did not lock
the skylight!"'
He shook his head.
"The gems, fossils, and gold may never be
found."

Muttson looked at his camera.
"Wait," he said, "I think the gems, fossils, and gold are still in the museum. Let us retrace our steps."

They followed Muttson back to the gem and mineral room.

"The case close to the wall was the one missing gems," Muttson said.

They followed Muttson back to the fossil room.
"The missing fish was also close to the wall,"
Muttson said.

They followed Muttson back to the American history room.
"The river is close to the same wall," said Muttson.
"And footprints go into a hole in the wall!"

"So what steals trinkets and lives inside a wall?" asked Furlock.

"It must be a pack rat," said Muttson.

"Of course!" said Mr. Leon.

"We know pack rats love bones and shiny things,"
said Muttson.
"Yikes!" Furlock squealed. "There it goes now!"

Furlock chased the pack rat.
Muttson and Mr. Leon chased Furlock.
"Stop, thief!" Furlock commanded. "You need
to return that fish fossil!"

"No way," said the pack rat.
"Why not move into the ancient midden?"
asked Muttson. "It was built by your
relatives."

"Okay," said the pack rat. "I do like all the
stuff you have here."
"Good idea," said Mr. Leon. "You will make our
display even more alive!"

Mr. Leon opened the midden and the pack rat
ran inside.
"I would like to thank you for your help," said
Mr. Leon.

"Would you take some cupcakes I made for the opening?" he asked.

"Yum!" said Furlock, and she gobbled one up.

"On thoo thuh neth caseth!" cried Furlock.

"I am right behind you," said Muttson.

They jumped into the Furlock-Mobile
and sped away.